OL' ST. NICK

RAVEN OAK

These stories are works of fiction. All of the characters and events portrayed in these stories are either productions of the authors' imaginations or are used fictitiously.

Ol' St. Nick

Copyright © 2015 by Raven Oak. All rights reserved. Originally published in *Joy to the Worlds: Mysterious Speculative Fiction for the Holidays* by Grey Sun Press.

2nd Edition, Copyright © 2021 by Raven Oak.

For information address Grey Sun Press, PO Box 1635 Bothell, WA 98041

WWW.GREYSUNPRESS.COM

ISBN 978-1-947712-01-0

Library of Congress Control Number: In Progress

The scanning, uploading, copying, and distribution of this book via the Internet or any other means without permission of the publisher is illegal and punishable by law. Please purchase authorized print or electronic editions. Participation in or encouragement of piracy of copyrighted materials hurts everyone. Your support of the arts is appreciated.

If you purchased this book without a cover, you should be aware that this book is stolen property. It was reported as "unsold and destroyed" to the publisher and neither the author nor the publisher has received any payments for this "stripped book."

Jolly Old Saint Nicholas,
Lean your ear this way;
Don't you tell a single soul
What I'm going to say,
Christmas Eve is coming soon;
Now my dear old man,
Whisper what you'll bring to me;
Tell me if you can.
When the clock is striking twelve,
When I'm fast asleep,
Down the chimney broad and black
With your pack you'll creep;
All the stockings you will find
Hanging in a row;
Mine will be the shortest one;
You'll be sure to know.

ORIGINAL LYRICS AS PUBLISHED
IN 1881

CHAPTER ONE

THE HOLE-RIDDLED SHIP reminded me of my Gran—broken and just a touch too old to remain in an ever-changing world. I'd seen many a battered ship, but standing on the bridge with nothing but a spacesuit between me and possible—scratch that, *probable*—death, set my stomach turning.

Two walls of the bridge were intact, though their computer displays—the undamaged ones, anyway—lay unresponsive. I floated near a hole as tall as me where something had ripped its way through the transport ship's shields and into the hull.

Treaty negotiations between Earth and the New Jhovens left union crews unwilling to contract with freelancers like me. That left my crew and I with salvage work like this. The creepiest kind of work.

Unsettling or not, this job was perfect. Honest theft as these folks had no need of their ship anymore. Besides, we needed the gig. If I had to stomach another protein bar for dinner, I'd be tempted to abandon my *own* damned ship.

Maybe it was *too* perfect. A ship that size, you'd expect

someone to miss her or at least miss her crew. If nothing else, word of the attack should have reached someone.

Yet the *Lucky Fish* stood empty—except for my meager crew who floated about scavenging for anything worth selling or using to repair my ship, *The Perffaith*.

Jake's shadow darkened the computer display in front of me. "Fight like this, makes me wonder if there's injured on board."

Half-fix-this, half-carry-that, Jake was my go-to man, though currently he was my *dig-for-parts* man as we combed the *Lucky Fish's* bridge.

"Body scans came up negative for life forms. If anyone's injured, they're long past needing our help, Jake."

"As we boarded, Lissa thought there might be unfriendlies on board. Maybe left over from the fight."

When I turned, his spacesuit's helmet light nailed me directly in the face. I winced, and he tapped a button at his wrist to dim it. "Sorry, Captain," he said.

"If you're that concerned, run another scan."

Jake shook his handheld. "Can't. Scanner's dead again."

No heat sources registered, not even ours, and I swore.

"There are all manner of species that don't read right on our scanners—*provided they work*—so no sense in being lax with security, sir."

I winced at his paraphrasing. "Remind me to give you the job if I ever need a new security officer. You nailed Lissa's deadpan perfectly." Her uptight personality used to be a boon. Now it was just a reminder of our past.

My suit's thick, synthetic fibers protected my fingers from the jagged metal hole in front of me. Jake pulled himself closer until he reached my side, his blond dreads mashed up against his sweaty face. "This is one battle I'm sure glad we missed."

Despite the fresh shave, my black scalp itched as sweat trickled down to my jaw. I glanced at Jake's dreads again.

"Itchy?" he asked.

"Yeah. Must be time to switch out the filters." Yet another thing to add to my growing list of repairs to make whenever we have money again.

"Maybe the *Lucky Fish* will have the parts." Jake's breathing was loud in my helmet's speakers. "I'm glad they ain't here. The stiffs, I mean. Hate when we hafta work around dead folks."

"Open channel two to *The Perffaith*," I spoke into my helmet, which buzzed in response. The channel light flipped to green, connecting me to my chief engineer. "Zac, any luck talking to the computer over here? Or getting her to power up?"

My helmet crackled, and when Zac answered, his voice was louder and clearer than before. "Nope. Something must've blown out the system. I'll need to hop on over to see what's the—"

"Negative, Zac. Remain on board *The Perffaith*." A press of my thumb and index finger closed the channel, and I flipped a power switch on a nearby console. No response. "Gut what you can, Jake. The bridge is a loss. But keep a lookout for the black box."

He removed the protective glass from a panel and set to stripping the innards of anything that didn't show obvious char-marks.

If I could find the black box, maybe I could sort out her last moments... The panel's door below me was fused together. I pushed away from it to float across to a more intact portion of the bridge. One console bore a few scorch marks but little else. The cover almost fell off in my hands, but its insides were a jumble of wires. No box.

"Open channel four." When the light lit, I asked, "Hey, Seb, how's it looking in the cargo hold?"

There was a delay in either the comm or his response.

Maybe the *Lucky Fish* was bouncing the signal around. Or maybe our suits sucked. I resisted the urge to rip off my helmet as static squealed in my ears and set them ringing.

"...Salvaged one crate...moved onto—"

"Did you catch any of that, Jake?"

Shoulder deep in computer hardware, he mumbled, "Said something 'bout salvaging a crate."

How helpful.

"Captain, we have an issue." Seb's voice rang too sharp in my ears.

"Report!"

"There is someone unexpected on the ship. A survivor perhaps."

The scanners had gone belly up again. Sweat rolled down my back, and the suit adjusted its humidity levels to compensate. "Where?"

"Unknown, Captain. The heat signature is sporadic."

"Zac—" There was no response on channel two. "Locate Officer Zac Curtis."

A squeal let loose in my helmet and channel five pulsed before autoconnecting. "Captain?"

"Why are you on a suit channel? Hurry up and shut the cargo doors on *The Perffaith*, Zac. I don't need anyone getting any ideas like making off with our ship."

"No-can-do, Captain. I just boarded the *Lucky Fish* to help track our mystery person."

Shit. No one could've survived on this ship full of holes. That left other scrappers. Folks likely to shoot first and ask questions later. At most, I figured we might run across some space critter or another—usually did on a salvage trip—but nothing humanoid or weapon-carrying.

But then, derelicts and wounded ships attracted the most unsavory types, didn't they?

No misplaced shadows lurked outside the bridge. I

snatched a serrated hunk of metal debris floating in front of me and shielded myself as I pushed my way along the corridor. Zac, my chief engineer, met me and Jake at the junction between Hallway A and Corridor C.

Zac gripped a piece of a wooden crate. He'd come from the left instead of the right, and I frowned.

Besides being an excellent engineer, the goofy guy had been my best friend since childhood. He must have guessed my thoughts as he said, "I rechecked the cargo hold on my way to you."

The corridor to engineering was as empty as those to the bridge had been. Outside the engine room, Lissa stood guard. The spacesuit hid her muscular frame, but she was imposing enough with the chill across her face.

"Jake, is Seb showing up on the scanner?" I asked. Jake slapped the device. "Is now."

"You and Zac intercept him. I don't want him tracking this heat source alone."

Both men pulled themselves down the corridor. I stuck my head inside the engine room. Two crew members were waist deep in engine parts. Too busy to notice anything but chipsets and circuitry.

I drifted back into the hall to Lissa, "Seen anything or anyone?"

"Nothing yet."

"Stay with the crew members here."

"But—"

I held up my hand and she *tsked*, something she did more often than I liked. Before she could voice her opinion, my speakers squawked. "Captain, we've got a problem."

"What is it, Zac?"

Silence made me hurry—as much as one could in a spacesuit.

More popping and sputtering from my speakers. Zac's

voice returned, halting my forward propulsion. "We found Seb. Damned heat source vanished."

"Vanished? Equipment malfunction?"

I'd replaced all the handheld scanners' memory chips last month. Cheap New Jhovensian shit.

"Worse. Our heat source is freshly dead."

CHAPTER TWO

THE ROOM SEB had discovered was little more than a closet. Crates and sacks of goods crowded it beyond cozy, and the dead body splayed through the center took up more than his fair share of space. His round belly floated over a thick, black belt cinching pants stained with grease and who knew what else. Then there was the garish red jacket. Ugly thing with too much fur for this century.

"He is freshly deceased, Captain. The body— " Seb's voice cracked, "—still bears warmth."

White whiskers were sprinkled across the dead man's broad chin, and his round cherry cheeks were rounder than I remembered. I forced my hand to relax around the hunk of debris I'd grabbed as a makeshift weapon.

Seb's white skin was near translucent as he hovered in the doorway. He was the only non-human on board, but with a pair of stylin' shades over his eyes and his orange afro wig, you could almost think him human. Right up 'til he opened his mouth and spewed something about the sins of freedom and enterprise in his near-perfect English.

He was the newest member of my crew—the most annoying member of my crew—but right now, I didn't blame him for getting a case of the wiggins.

Petrie, my medical officer, squeezed past him. Her hip brushed his leg, and Seb flinched. "Back away from the body, please," said Petrie. She crouched with a grunt as the crew watched. A sour smell left my tongue too thick in my mouth.

"You good, Cap?" asked Zac.

I blinked several times to clear my head. "Unnecessary complications bug me is all."

"So what happened to him, Doc?"

Petrie glanced at Zac, then returned her attention to the victim. "I'll need to do a full autopsy to be sure, but I suspect he asphyxiated."

"What's the scanner say about that heat source now, Zac? If someone on board killed this man, it's not too far a stretch to think they might kill someone else," I said.

He held up his scanner. The blue grid held a dozen heat sources, every last one of them traceable to the trackers in our suits.

Seb glared at the functioning scanner. "I followed the foreign heat source here before it disappeared. This tells me the man who appeared as an additional heat source is the one lying before us."

"Ya really think someone offed him, Mark? I mean, ship's pretty damaged—what's one more stiff on a ship like this?" Jake asked.

Our dead man lacked a beard the last time I saw him. I blinked away the memory and said, "There's something odd about this whole thing. Between the body, the sensors... This man was alive before we boarded, but how? There's no space-suit. No air."

"So how'd he breathe? You're right, Cap. Something stinks," said Zac.

"Murder or not, we'll make a full sweep of the *Lucky Fish*." I opened a channel to Lissa. "Get the crew and whatever they salvaged over to *The Perffaith*, then join me in canvassing the *Lucky Fish's* bow. And keep your eyes open."

"Roger that."

"Zac, Seb, search the stern. I'll work from the bridge back."

Both frowned. "I would best seek with you, Captain."

"You're with Zac, Seb."

"But—"

Zac petted Seb on the shoulder. "Don't sweat it. Captain here works best *without* our advice. You'll get used to it."

I flicked Zac on the shoulder, though with my gloves it came out more a tap. I caught his grimace before it disappeared behind his gloved hand.

"I do not understand."

"Give it time. You'll learn to love this ship and its crazy crew once you've been here a while. We rib each other—which means we joke a lot. I know your people aren't so much with the jokes, but you'll adjust," I said. With a nod to Zac, we set out to hunt for a possible survivor...or murderer. Between the debris and bulky spacesuits—I couldn't afford the good stuff— the search was slow going. Other than a few bodies that hadn't been wrenched into space during the fight, no original crewmen remained on the *Lucky Fish*. Our lone heat source was our closeted corpse.

It was a crime worth blowing off, but something nagged me about it. When I returned to the crime scene, a quick search turned up an ID, though I gave it little more than a glance. It was probably fake. Five years and a funny outfit didn't hide those green eyes any more than they hid the scars along his face from one too many brawls.

I dimmed my helmet's visor, blocking out my father's face. It shouldn't have bothered me. We hadn't seen each other in years, and it wasn't like I gave two shits about him. I couldn't afford the distraction. Nevertheless, my jaw ached as I guarded his body. Lissa found me a few minutes later.

"Mark, are you all right?"

"Open channel one—private seal." When the green light inside my helmet flickered, I said to Lissa, "Check out the doorway."

She took a moment to study the frame, stopping near the latch. "The door was pried open."

I pointed at one mark in particular. Paint chips remained embedded in the metal. "Blue paint. *Our* blue paint."

She frowned. "You don't know that for a fact."

"Who else uses Cadmium Blue #20 to label their tools? That's not the normal color used out here. Freelancers Guild uses Cedar Green #8 by and large."

Her gloved fingers flicked a large paint chip from the gouge and sent it drifting into an open bag she held. "It's a common paint color, Captain. For other things at least."

Two channels lit amber in my helmet's display. "Release privacy status," I said and spotted Zac floating toward us with Seb a foot behind.

"Captain, ship's clear as clear can be," said Zac. Seb confirmed the clear status with a nod.

Lissa handed me the key card to the victim's room.

Someone—probably me—was gonna get to dig through his belongings.

"I know I asked before, but are you okay, Mark? You look... shaken," she said.

I turned from that look, a look that wasn't hers to give anymore. Text on the card said Room 5, Level 3. No power meant no lift, so I set out for the emergency stairs. I used the railing to pull myself up until my helmet lamp shined on the number three. When I paused in my ascent, I caught Lissa trailing behind me. "You didn't have to come along."

"You're searching the room."

"Someone has to."

"How do we know it's his room?"

I shrugged. "Not sure, but if nothing else, I'd like to know why he carried the key card."

As we stopped outside room five, I took a deep breath. Like the closet-sized room we'd found him in, the door had been forced open. Pry marks made by something metal had left regular indentations on it. *Unlike* his final resting place, no blue paint chips marred these. I pointed this out to Lissa before we stepped inside.

A fold-up cot filled the majority of the room. Five wall-drawers shared space with a pull-out sink and toilet bowl.

Typical traveler's quarters. I almost laughed to think of someone as flamboyant and crass as Nick living out of a room like this.

I would've figured he'd opt for a suite.

My light reflected off something on the floor, and I rotated upside down to retrieve it. Glass. "Give me a hand," I muttered, and Lissa gave my legs a push 'til I got upright.

"What is it?"

I held it up to our eye level. "Looks like a snow globe. Used to have one of these as a kid." Small, white dust swirled around inside the glass dome and glittered in my light.

She held up an old paperback just as Zac and Seb crossed through the doorway.

"Is that an honest-to-god real book?" asked Zac.

I nodded and set the glass object on the cot. "Real paper, too. I take it your search is done?"

"Yep. Na-da-thing on board but us."

Lissa passed the book to Zac, and he gasped at the cover. "It's our victim!" On the cover, a fat man in a red suit grinned at us. "The Tale of Jolly Ol' Saint Nicholas. Some old artifact from Earth, maybe?"

As much as I hated to admit it, the saint did bear a certain cheesy resemblance to our victim. It was uncanny the way those same green eyes stared back at me, and for a moment, I was a child again and running.

Always running.

"Captain, look." Zac pointed to some text on the front page. "Says here this Saint Nicholas man was some special dignitary on Earth way back when."

There was a cough in my ears. Seb and Jake crowded around the door, hanging on every word Zac uttered as he continued to ramble on about some long dead holiday where folks exchanged gifts and sang about happier times.

"That body isn't a saint. Certainly not some gift-giver," I muttered.

The chatter around me ceased, and Zac cocked his head. "How you figure? Looks like the real deal—the real Santa Claus—to me."

My brain caught up with my mouth. "Too many scars on him. That man's seen too many brawls to be some cheerful saint. I mean, aren't saints supposed to be holy or something?"

Seb asked, "But how would you explain his attire? It is identical to that on the book."

Damn him. The *Alphan* latched onto anything like it was gospel truth. A habit I'd have to break if he wished to remain first mate.

Seb continued, "He even possesses a—what did you call it, Zac? A traditional gift?"

"What gift?"

"The snow globe and book. A find like this might be worth some coin." Zac's eyes glittered in my helmet's light.

"Should we not be worried about how this saint died?" Seb shook the snow globe I'd cast aside earlier, sending white flutters around the tiny city inside.

My stomach threatened to empty itself right there in all

that junk. From simple salvage to a crime scene, this job was everything I'd hoped to avoid. Including seeing my father, Nick. Either way, I wasn't gonna be able to walk away without the answer to at least one question: What the hell had Nick been doing on this ship?

CHAPTER THREE

"ACCORDING TO HIS IDENTIFICATION, the victim's name is Nick Johnson."

Banes, not Johnson. My brain corrected the details. Why'd he choose Gran's maiden name for his false persona? I ground my teeth as the crew crowded around the body like voyeurs. Petrie, my chief medical officer, rattled more information from her examination as the infirmary display scrolled with data.

Petrie continued, "Until we're able to access the derelict's computer, we won't be able to ascertain his purpose on the *Lucky Fish*. Maybe he's following the old Earth myth of Santa Claus." Eyes the color of weak tea twinkled, lending beauty to an otherwise plain face. "The team found a sack full of Earth artifacts stowed in a crate in the cargo hold."

Knowing Nick, the goods were probably stolen. I swallowed back bile.

"The identification plate on the crate's side matches that of our victim." Petrie pulled back the sheet to expose Nick's face. The swollen, red skin marred the sterile and clinical white room. Like someone had opened a can of animal innards and maraschino cherries, molded them Nick-shaped, and plopped them down on the table.

Lissa's shoulder muscles strained against her blue shirt as she leaned over the victim. She held back her long red braids with one hand and pointed at a pinprick in his neck with the other. "Is this how he died?" she asked.

Petrie pointed again at the large display panel. Scans of various organs scrolled by with a ton of numbers that meant nothing to me. "His toxicology screens show he suffered anoxia—"

At our blank stares, she added, "He asphyxiated as a result of exposure to carbon monoxide."

"When? Seb said we had a heat signature," I interrupted. "The victim was alive when we hailed the *Lucky Fish* and found their computer unresponsive. He died within ten minutes of our coming aboard, so where'd he get the CO exposure?"

"And what about this injection or pinprick cut?" asked Lissa.

"Coincidental. Something done prior to death."

I ran a finger over the tiny wound. "You sure, Petrie?"

"Yes, Captain. Cause of death is anoxia."

Behind me, Seb and Zac whispered over the death of *Santa Claus*. Speculation bred rumors, and I shushed them. "Can you tell me how he survived without a ship suit? Was there air in that room?"

"In some areas, oxygen was present and cycling after whatever fight left holes in the *Lucky Fish*." Petrie's eyes narrowed. "You look like you have another question."

"Yeah, which one of us killed him?" You'd have thought I'd sucked the air from our ship the way Seb gasped. "Do the math, Seb."

I couldn't see his eyes behind those enormous sunglasses he wore, nor did his mouth-flap tilt to indicate comprehension.

Seb held up his hands. "There is no math to complete. I assume this is another idiom?"

The only non-Earthling on board, and he spoke better English than me. Toss him a saying, and he'd be chewing on it for the next hour. "Think about it. Victim died of...anoxia, but that room itself took no damage. Air was circulating. So how'd he die?"

Zac asked, "Airflow controller ain't on the fritz, is it?"

"Sensors would've picked up the increase throughout the ship."

"Not with all them holes, Captain." Zac frowned. "Wasn't any air to check. It'd all been sucked out."

Lissa leaned against the wall, arms crossed and eyes narrowed. "Airflow controller was one of the salvaged parts. Booted up just fine for Zac's lackey," she said.

Nick had been right. Damned fool had been destined to die in space. Not that he hadn't had it coming. He was an asshole at best and mobster at worst.

"I wonder if it was a safe room. Pretty common on passenger ships, and it would explain why the room had its own circulation system," said Lissa.

"Maybe this Santa felt all dizzy or something from CO buildup. Messed up and took the wrong drugs? Maybe he went and shot himself up with something that later killed him? Something that interacted with CO levels?" Jake asked.

An interesting idea, but I shook my head.

"Captain?"

I wrested my glance from the stiff.

"Mr. Johnson received a dose of adrenaline sometime before death. If it had been fatal, his heart muscles would display signs of stress, of pumping harder," Petrie explained. "His blood work would show the increase of adrenaline or the chemicals found in whatever drug he could've taken, but nothing showed up in my preliminary tests. The dose he received was too small to do much of anything. Certainly not kill him."

I tapped my gold sliver of a wristband. "Bridge." Once connected I asked, "Did our sensors pick up any trace signatures when we approached the *Lucky Fish?* Like someone leaving as we arrived?"

The crew member on duty answered in the negative, then asked, "Would you like me to run a second analysis of the scans to be sure?"

"Yes, and send the report to my inbox." To my officers, I said, "Maybe the injection was a trick. Something to make us look the other way or ignore his death altogether."

My crew stared at each other, taking turns to weigh suspicions and prejudices. It was comical in a way, made more so by the stripes of pungent cinnamon paste under their noses.

The wall display read 21:04. A long day that would only get longer if I was gonna figure out who knocked off Nick. "Zac and Seb, I want a complete report on the airflow controller and any other parts on the *Lucky Fish* that might explain this. Petrie, run your tests, and Lissa, start looking into what crew may or may not have had ties with our victim. We'll meet at 02:00 in the common area."

Five people I trusted stood around a dead myth until Petrie zipped the mesh bag closed. My officers left the room individually—none of them wishing to turn their back on another.

Not that I blamed them.

Alone with the doc, I said, "Petrie-Dish, I don't want to jump to any conclusions, but I think someone from my crew killed him."

With a glance at the emptying hallway, she leaned close to my ear. "Don't tell a single one of them what I'm going to say, but I agree. You were on the *Lucky Fish* for twenty minutes before we found Mr. Johnson. Based on the body's lack of lividity, he was deceased for approximately ten minutes when Seb found him. He died right under our noses."

"The room was sealed until one of us pried it open, Petrie. It had its own air circulation, but someone tinkered with it."

She wrinkled her nose, but not at any smell in the infirmary. "Then we're all suspects at this point. Someone did something to cause the buildup of carbon monoxide. Question is, was it intentional? I'll run more tests."

She slid the metal tray bearing Nick into the wall and closed the door. The unit locked with a beep after she pressed her hand to the frontal display screen. "Captain, don't take this the wrong way, but something odd did show up in my autopsy."

I tilted my head but said nothing.

"I ran a print scan, and this Nick Johnson, he doesn't exist. There is no record on file."

I allowed the breath I'd been holding to seep out in a slow exhale. "He must be a criminal then. Any record of such things?"

"Captain, when I say there's no record, I mean it. He's a ghost." The stringent odor of antiseptics hit me as she lathered her arms up to the elbow. "I'll run DNA, but that will take time."

My insides trembled. "Keep digging," I said and fled the infirmary.

Once in my quarters, I leaned against the door as my body shook. I wasn't certain why I was hiding Nick's identity; whether it was for his good or my own, I couldn't be sure, but they couldn't know.

They didn't need to know because *I* didn't kill my father.

I dug through a wall-drawer for a tattered box hidden in the back. I wrestled it from beneath a pair of old boots and set it on my desk. At first, I merely stared at it, but as the silence settled around me like his red cloak, I lifted the lid off the memories.

Nick's face stared at me from the digital photo, his cheeks pink from the mountain's snow. What began as a sigh left me curled in a ball like a child.

I didn't love him—hell, I didn't know him—but now I never would.

CHAPTER FOUR

I HADN'T MEANT to doze.

The report on the *Lucky Fish*'s circulation system confirmed that the air system was fully operational up until the time of death. Someone from my crew had to have tampered with it. After reading this and grinding my teeth at the implications, I'd dozed until something woke me.

A door rattle wasn't normally the type of noise I'd notice, but my sleep had been uneasy and light. Dreams about the day Nick had left, and Gran shouting at him and cursing his name. Seeing her again, even in dreams, left me brittle.

The bleary wall-clock struck midnight, and thumping footfalls paused outside then continued on.

The door panel glowed blue at my approach. "Display heat sources in corridor A," I whispered. One figure moved toward the common area. It wasn't unusual to see folks moving about, but something in my gut told me to follow. The door hissed open as I left my quarters in pursuit.

The creeping figure ahead wore all black and carried a sack tossed over their shoulder. The overhead lights, dimmed for nighttime, cast jagged shadows, and I cursed the lack of foresight that left me weaponless. A door ten feet ahead opened and closed in rapid succession.

When I approached, the door slid open a second time, bathing me in light. Too much light for the common area. Rather than their normal white, the overhead lights twinkled in reds and golds to the rhythm of an odd thump, and I held up a hand to block the glare. "What in all hells—"

"My apologies, Captain. I was testing their luminosity. Allow me to decrease the illumination." Seb's hairless eyebrows danced above heavily darkened lenses the size of my fist. He dropped the bag on the table before he set about adjusting the lights on a handheld control screen.

"Seb, I don't mean you any insult, but what in the world are you doing in here carrying—" I riffled through the bag. "— A bag of socks?"

He slid a sealed box of thumbtacks across the table. "Once I completed my report on the airflow controller, I researched the mythos of Santa Claus. With one of his servants on board, I thought it might help us through our turmoil if we carried on with our own good cheer."

"Good cheer? During a murder? What are you talking about, Seb? That man isn't Santa—"

He shook out the lengthier socks before tacking them to the wall above the baseboard ventilation shaft. "Captain, I am aware of these facts, but we have a murderer among us. That is not something I wish to dwell on. Instead, I will hang these stockings by the chimney with care—"

"Stop." Another sock dangled between his fingers, this one bearing blue and green stripes, and I asked, "Why are you nailing socks to my ship's walls?"

"In the mythos of Earth's Christmas, Earthlings suspended stockings from chimneys in order to summon the great Saint Nicholas. Also, it is possible they protect against dust bunnies. Are dust bunnies a common fear among Earthlings?"

He hung two more socks on the wall, and I shook my head. "You realize he's a myth, right? Santa Claus isn't real. Neither are dust bunnies for that matter."

Seb continued his "decorating" until ten socks hung from the wall—one for each of my crew—though one sock dangled half the length of the others.

"What's with the short one?" I asked.

"Have you ever heard of *gherblins*?" I shook my head. "Sometimes *gherblins* creep onto the ship at night and steal the socks my mother knits. When my socks no longer possess a mate, I stow them in a box to send home."

"So what? You shrank one?"

Seb shook his head. "After we ferried that group from Yabanc last year, someone left the miniature stocking in the cargo bay. I suspect one of their offspring may have mislaid it."

He slung the empty bag across his shoulder. His mouth-flap split, both top lips forming a half-grin. Coupled with his sunglasses and unusually pale skin, it painted a grotesque picture. My skin crawled like I'd walked through a cobweb. "Is there anything else you require, Captain?" Seb asked.

I wanted to tell him, explain why I was bothering with Nick. I mean, he was my first mate. I should've been able to trust him. Instead, I shrugged it off. "I hate complications."

"That is completely understandable." Seb turned away from the door frame as he continued to decorate.

"Someone killed that man, and I gotta ask, Seb, why do this in the middle of the night? Did it ever occur to you that I might've thought you the murderer? Might still?"

His bushy orange wig escaped his hood when he laughed. "Me? Kill Santa? I am not the one experienced in dead bodies."

"Petrie? Why suspect her?"

"Why not? We are all capable of horrible deeds, are we not? Even you, I suspect."

Yes, I am.

He mistook my silence and said, "No offense intended, Captain." As he sauntered from the room, fro first, I remained alone with blinking lights and empty stockings, both of which chased my thoughts in circles. Petrie had been on my ship during the murder, or so I'd thought. Besides, no way a woman like her would know a crook like Nick, much less have a reason to kill him. Or so I thought.

As much as I didn't want to admit it, Petrie *did* have access to all manner of medicines and the knowledge to cover up the crime. It wouldn't be the first time Nick had steered a new crew member my way in order to set me up. It was time to find out what Ol' Nick had been up to in the years since I'd last seen him.

I swore as I trudged back to my quarters. Nothing good would come of this business with Ol' Saint Nick.

But then, nothing ever had.

CHAPTER FIVE

THE SECTOR'S trace report noted no fewer than five ships in the area before our arrival, but none of them during Nick's murder. Just my ship, *The Perffaith*. Without access to the *Lucky Fish*'s computer, a spacewalk in a black hole would've been easier than tracing Nick's movements. Zac could've helped, being my local computer expert, but at this point, I didn't trust anyone.

Sad truth was, I wanted to trust them all.

The last time I'd seen Nick, he'd been on Europa running "errands" for Junto, the father of Europa's crime family. I pecked at the handheld screen, which glared in the darkness until I swiped a finger down the side to dim it. A search of his name pulled up a list of warrants, arrest records, and bounties. His current address showed up as unknown. Not exactly surprising, especially if he were still working for Junto.

We'd last met in his shack on Europa. Too much condensation and not enough filtration had left the walls a pattern of black and green splotches, and my nose twitched at the memory. The business card he'd given me that day—*Raymond*

Royant, Antiquities Dealer—had a relay code which I now keyed in. Error messages scrolled across the screen.

"No such contact. Would you like to execute a last known trace-run?"

I hit the "no" button and leaned my head against the wall. How do you find a guy who lives off the grid?

A green light blinked on my handheld. "Incoming Call—Unknown Number."

"Accept call," I said. No picture appeared—just an empty, black screen.

"Whosit?" a gruff voice asked.

"Since you called, you tell me. By any chance, is this Raymond—"

"I asked you a question, boy. Whosit?"

I cleared my throat. "Um, this is Mark Banes. If this is Raymond, I met you once with Nick—"

The black screen fizzled a moment until Raymond's grumpy face appeared. If I hadn't known any better, I'd have sworn he'd been wearing that same flannel shirt when I'd met him a few years' back. Bloodshot eyes glared at me above a week's worth of stubble. He sat cross-legged in some shack whose walls were lined with cardboard, and he smacked his screen when it grew fuzzy. "I get ya. Yer that turd who left yer dad when he's all sick and shit. Rat bastard's who ya are."

I rolled my eyes visibly, even for a bad connection. "Look, I'm not here to argue his merits or lack of them with you. I just wanna know where he is." I knew the answer, but I was hoping that lying would get me a trail of where he'd been.

"Nick left."

"When?"

"I dunno. Do I look like his secretary? Damn bitch was hot, too. Hotter than me." Raymond took a swig from a bottle he'd been storing between his knees. "Yer hair's shorter than that time you visited Nick."

I ran a hand over my brown head. "He still working for Junto?"

Raymond flinched but nodded. The screen flickered then went dark, and the dissonant tritone of a disconnect assaulted my ears.

The last time I'd seen my father, he'd given me some song and dance about being terminal. It wasn't the first time I'd heard that line of bull. Nick's one skill was looking out for number one—that was him. Whether he'd owed Junto's boys money or had bought into some get-rich-quick-scheme, he'd come running to Gran and me when he was low on cash. Or booze. Or both.

And I'd run just a little bit further into space and away from him.

I thought I'd run far enough. Seems as though he'd found a way to run to me.

CHAPTER SIX

NICK'S DEATH, the reality that he'd had cancer, and my lack of sleep left me with visions of drunken bums dancing in my head like a bad 3D flick while I contemplated calling Junto. I had a good hour before the 02:00 meeting with the crew. With a heavy sigh, I put in the call to the Callisto Space Station.

I'd repeated my request to five lackeys before I reached someone physically stationed on Europa, then to another lackey before reaching the Family proper. "I know you don't wanna tick off your boss, but see, he owes me one," I said to the funny little man on my screen. His mustache—if one could call a pencil-thin line scribbled above one's upper lip an actual mustache—twitched. "Tell him Captain Mark Banes would like to call in a favor."

The screen went a hazy, snowy gray for another minute or two before the man himself appeared. He'd lost a good fifty pounds since I'd last seen him, and his comb-over was more wilt than comb. I grinned like we were old friends. "How's life in the Family, Junto? You're looking good."

He didn't return my smile but wagged a thin finger at me. "Where is he?"

"Where's who?"

Junto leaned so close to his screen that his nose near bumped against it. "Your father, who do ya think? Son-of-a-bitch nicked some priceless antiquities from...a client. He was s'posed to deliver them to me, but he got all chicky. Took off with the goods."

"Nick's anything but a coward." My left eye twitched, and I tried to ignore it.

"There's somethin' you ain't tellin' me. Now I know I owe you a favor, which I'm willing to make good on, but I can't help you if you're lyin' to me."

"Let me guess. This is what he stole." I held up the snow globe. This time, his nose touched his screen, and I got a shot of more nose hairs than I needed.

"Where is he? Don't make me—"

"He's dead."

Junto's lips tilted up at the corners.

So he already knew that, did he? I continued fishing. "Found him dead on a beat-up ship out here in the Theros cluster. What was Nick doing on the *Lucky Fish?*"

"I assume hidin' from me."

"And it's just a coincidence that I happened upon him?"

Junto leaned away from the screen for a moment of whispering with some shadow in the background before he returned. "Look Mark, I'll tell you what I know, because we're...friends, but after this we're square. I won't owe you shit. Got it?"

It wasn't a fair trade, and the rat bastard knew it. "Fine. Tell me everything."

"Normally Nick made good on his deals, one way or another, but sometimes he gots to thinkin' he could skip the middle man. Took off with that globe-thingy you got, some honest-to-god books—"

I cut him off. "I mean no offense, Junto, but I already know what he took. Get to the bit about him being all corpsified on the *Lucky Fish*."

Junto's eyes narrowed. "My sources say he'd fooled that captain into thinkin' he was more than some two-credit con artist." He waited for me to react, and when I merely shrugged, he asked, "What? No love for *honest* Nick?"

"Say what you want. He *was* a con man. I've got no warm fuzzies for him."

"Raymond's right. You're quite the bastard. I like it!" Junto laughed with his arms wrapped around a much smaller gut. "Once I found his hidin' spot, I sent some of my boys to recover the goods."

"You sure that was all they were there to do?"

"If I wanted Nick dead, there's all manner of folks I coulda sent. I wanted the loot. That's it."

I shook the snow globe before the screen. "I assume the goods are valuable. Why'd your boys leave without them?"

"Fool captain of the *Lucky Fish* believed Nick. Can you imagine? Thought your old man was some freakin' saint or some shit. Captain refused to give me what I was owed, so my boys got...messy. Ship was in pieces when they boarded. Weren't any trace of Nick or the goods."

"You didn't look very hard."

Junto smiled into the screen. "You know everything I do."

He was lying. If he'd wanted the goods, he'd have taken them. Or asked me to fetch them seeing how I was holding them. I wouldn't push a man like Junto too hard—doing so would only result in my death if I were lucky, and the deaths of my entire crew if I were not—but I could certainly play a little.

"Seeing as how you've gone and lost your goods, what's in it for me to return them? I could part—"

Junto severed the connection before I'd finished. While I had the *why* to Nick's appearance on the *Lucky Fish*, it didn't tell me who had killed him or their reasoning. Junto's boys had been long gone by the time Nick had asphyxiated.

I swiped a hand across my screen to lock it. I'd hoped it would be unnecessary, but maybe the search among my crew would yield more answers. At a minimum, we'd start with interviews.

I hoped my crew was in a truthful mood.

CHAPTER SEVEN

BEFORE I COULD SHADOW my eyes from the twinkling lights, Lissa's pile of braids blocked the brightness. "Morning, Captain." She resumed her pacing while she gestured towards the seat awaiting me.

The rest of my crew straddled benches along either side of the table. Bags drooped beneath most eyes, and no one paid any mind to the socks tacked to the back wall.

"It's not even 02:00 yet," I muttered and hooked a stool leg with my foot. When it scraped across the floor, Seb flinched and sent a splash of red sludge over his mug's rim. "Everyone's a mite jumpy this early morning."

Lissa cleared her throat. "Not surprising given the circumstances and lack of sleep."

"Fair enough. I did a little digging about our corpse. Seems he had a run in with Junto and the Family."

"Our stiff was a mobster? Cool." Jake threw up his hands at my glare. "Or not cool. Shame on him. Bad Mr. Santa Mobster."

I rapped my knuckles on the table. "Enough. Junto's boys were long gone when we arrived, so they weren't the killers.

Someone on *my* ship murdered Sant—I mean, Mr. Johnson. Maybe it was self-defense. Maybe it was spur of the moment or even an accident. Either way, we got a corpse on our hands and not a whole lotta answers."

"Are we sure it was one of us?" Lissa asked, and I nodded.

"Analysis says we were the only ship within three hours of the *Lucky Fish* at the time of death. Someone on *The Perffaith* killed him. I want everyone interviewed, Lissa. Where they were, what they were doing—report to me by noon."

"There is not any need, Captain." When Seb stood, his eyes hiding behind oval frames, my gut played a round of slug-it-out with my esophagus. "I think we know who our killer is."

Many feet shuffled beneath the table. "Considering we don't have much more than a mob connection and an autopsy, I find that surprising, Seb."

Zac whispered, "The autopsy. It would be easy to—"

"To what? Lie? Break my oath? Is that what you're suggesting?" asked Petrie. Her end of the bench slid sideways as she rose to her feet. When she leaned across the table toward Zac, Lissa's hand on my arm stopped my own forward motion.

"Might as well see what shakes loose. This has been brewing all morning," Lissa said.

Without so much as a glance in our direction, Seb said, "Peter, I—"

"It's pronounced Pe-tree, not Pe-ter."

"Petrie then. You cannot deny how easy it would be for you to doctor an autopsy. You have access to needles and medicines we do not, and—"

For all her plain looks, Petrie's height made for an imposing figure as she leaned close enough to kiss Seb. The tips of her shoulder length hair bounced off his chin, and he flushed to match the blinking red lights. "Why would I risk my career to kill a stranger?"

"It is not my business to say."

"Don't think I don't know, Seb."

She broke eye contact when I knocked my fist on the table. "Enough double-speak. If you know something, either of you, get to it. Otherwise, sit down and shut up. We've got better ways to spend our time."

"Seb's been spying on me. Late at night when he thinks no one's watching," said Petrie, and Seb hissed.

"Why would he do that?" I asked.

Lissa, who had been calm a moment before, paled. Petrie reached out to grip Lissa's shoulder. "Lissa and I are together. A couple. *Alphans* are not known for their tolerance of...well..."

I closed my eyes. Onboard relationships—damned things never ended well. At best they fizzled out, and at worst, they burned a hole through the ship. A picture of the *Lucky Fish's* bridge came to mind.

Beside me, Lissa was a confident woman who wore her strength physically as well as mentally. My chief medical officer—Petrie-Dish Extraordinaire as I called her —was an old friend but the complete antithesis of Lissa. Petrie embraced her curves like she had middle age, with shy apologies. The idea of Lissa hooking up with someone suffering under insecurities made little sense to me.

But then, nothing about the past twelve hours made any sense.

Petrie bit her lip as she awaited my response.

"As a general rule, I dislike onboard relationships. However, I see no reason for concern here. What Petrie and Lissa do in their spare time is their own business," I said.

Seb's shoulders slumped forward as Petrie turned away from him. If his mouth-flap could've frowned, it would've. Lissa kept herself angled between him and Petrie, and her finger brushed the taser clipped to her belt.

"Lissa will interview folks, then I'll interview her. She'll send me the reports by noon."

"I'd suggest we search rooms as well," said Lissa.

I waved a hand at her. We weren't there—*yet*. There had to be an easier explanation to this than murder.

"And who gets to interview you, Mark?" asked Zac.

It was Lissa who answered. "I will."

"But what if you two are in cahoots? I hate to suggest it, but if we're all suspects, we're *all* suspects. Besides, you two have a somewhat colorful past."

Zac was right. I hated when he was right. I rubbed my temples and answered, "You can all interview me. Fair?"

"Whatever you say, Captain."

The edge to his voice confused me. I glanced around the table only to be met by furrowed brows and deep frowns. Trouble was brewing like a solar flare. Whatever was happening, I was gonna have to deal with it quickly.

CHAPTER EIGHT

THE SECOND RUN of *The Perffaith*'s sensors showed the majority of my crew on the *Lucky Fish* as they should've been, the exceptions being Zac and Petrie. Sensors indicated both had left *The Perffaith* when Seb had spotted the heat source. That aside, I awaited the rest of the reports with a spinning mind and stomach.

Another blip—this one from Petrie—pinged my inbox before noon. I don't know what I'd expected the medical report to tell me beyond what I already knew—carbon monoxide poisoning, adrenaline injection, blah-blah medical jargon—but her write-up gave an alarmingly accurate portrayal of Nick's life. I reread the last paragraph twice to be sure I'd gotten it right.

Liver cirrhosis indicates a heavy drinker. Scarring of the lungs and esophageal tissue indicates heavy tobacco use. No indications of drug use in the blood or tissue. Five cysts, 2 cm. in size, were removed from the lungs, and two 1 cm cysts were removed left of the trachea. Tests revealed these cysts to be malignant in nature. Patient probably suffered from Stage

IV lung cancer at the time of death. No evidence of standard or unusual cancer treatment (radiation, stem cell placement, etc.) was found.

Damn. My old man hadn't been lying after all. I closed the report and put in a call to Zac.

He stood beside a pile of scanners, their motherboards spread out across the table. "Whatcha need, Captain?"

"Meet me in the captain's station in five minutes."

He nodded as I closed the call and left my room. As I walked to the bridge I passed Jake, who stared at his shoes. No one on the bridge paid me any mind. Once the door to the captain's station slid shut, I settled in behind my desk and pulled up my recent research.

"Officer Zac Curtis requests entry," the computer announced a few moments later.

"Approve."

The door slid open, and Zac stepped inside. "I figured you'd call me down sooner or later." When I cocked an eyebrow, he added, "I've done all I can to try and salvage the *Lucky Fish*'s computer, but the data's too dang damaged—"

"That's not why I called you here."

I tapped the screen beside me and angled it to give him a better view. The picture of Nick and me was old, but it didn't take Zac longer than an exhale to make the connection.

His mouth fell open, then closed, and then opened again. "I assume you plan on telling me why you went and took a picture with Santa?"

I nodded. "You remember a few years back when my old man sent me a message saying he was dying?"

"Yeah, but—wait, *that* Nick is *this* Nick?" He squinted at the screen. "Whoa. Last time I saw his raggedy ass we were both still kids and your Gran was tossing him out for drinking again. When'd he get so old?"

I closed the image with a shrug. "Years bouncing from place to place, doing odd jobs for Junto and his boys will age someone quick enough." I pulled up Petrie's autopsy report. "Petrie says he was dying. Cancer."

Zac let out a low whistle. "So he wasn't scamming you last time, huh?"

"Apparently not. Though it doesn't explain who killed him."

"Or why you're keeping this info secret from everyone," said Zac.

"What happened between me and Nick in the past...is personal, and you'll keep this information to yourself for the time being. It'll only make waves, and the last thing we need is more tension."

Zac nodded, but his fingers toyed with the buttons on his shirt. "You know they'll think it's you. Especially if they discover the damage between you two."

I pulled up the last email I'd received from Nick. "I can't help that. It wasn't me—I've got no reason to kill him."

"Except that he abandoned you and your ma, and later your Gran. Hell, left your Gran with quite the debt if I recall. Then he left you with nothing more than a dream of what a dad's s'posed to be. Sounds like a pretty damned good reason to me."

Zac scanned the email on the screen. "You went to see him?" When I nodded, Zac asked, "Why?"

"Curiosity mainly. You know me well enough to know that I wouldn't kill him, no matter how much I hated him. The others don't. Especially Seb. He's new to the crew and wouldn't understand."

I didn't imagine the scowl on Zac's face, but like a flickering screen it blinked away a second later. "Why'd you go and pick him up, anyway? Nothing against his people, but it's uncanny the way he looks at us. Like we're dinner."

Another report scrolled across my screen. This one an addendum from Lissa on which crew had kin ties to the Europan Family. Only one name popped up, an engineer in Zac's department whose great-great-great grandmother married an ex-mobster. The details blurred before my eyes. "Junto."

"You took on that freak for your first mate for Junto?" Rather than his usual laughter, Zac's nostrils flared slightly.

"He arranged for some of the more...lucrative jobs to come our way in exchange for my accepting Seb on board as first mate. It's complicated, and we needed the cash. What can you tell me about Jelgins?" I asked.

"Engineer?" Zac rubbed his jaw. "Seems stable enough. Why? Peg him for the murderer or something?"

"Lissa found a tie with the Family—"

"His great-something-or-other, right?" Zac snorted. "He's no more a mobster than I am. Though Seb, you know he's reporting back to Junto."

I closed the report without responding to his comment. "I need you to hack into Nick's email account."

"What email client does he use?"

"M-net."

"Of course. It's free. Shouldn't be too hard."

My best friend tapped a few buttons and once at the client, he clicked the login button and typed a long word into the password field. One keystroke later, Nick's email scrolled across the screen.

"Easy password."

"That *was* easy. What was it?"

He rolled his eyes at me. "Your full name."

CHAPTER NINE

ZAC LEFT me alone with the emails and my thoughts, neither of which were any good. The man had barely said more than a dozen words to me (when he wasn't asking for money that was), but had used my name for his password. It left me unsettled as I crawled through messages from Junto and his boys. The majority were little more than an address and a date and time. Damned fool didn't delete anything. Must've driven Junto crazy with all his rules on security and traceability.

Three screens in had gotten me nowhere. Rather than spin my wheels on mob business, I pulled up a search to compare Nick's account with the names and email addresses of my crew. The computer made short work of my search, and the name that popped up, wasn't the name I'd expected.

Over a dozen messages linked Lissa to my father, the earliest made two years prior. The first inquired about the murder of Melinda Mathis-Kerric. I made a note to look into it and kept reading. Lissa's emails to my father grew more insistent, first a short inquiry and when Nick revealed his usual non-caring self, she pointed fingers at Junto, the mob, and finally Nick.

The last message asked to meet, and the date lined up with some vacation time Lissa had taken a few months back. Nothing further appeared in the search, and I typed in a request for emails to Junto on the same date. One result appeared.

> *Received: by 10.93.34.126.43.122*
> *with SSIMTP id 3927be492;*
> *Saturday, February 8, 2106*
> *03:45:21 (-7 Standard Time)*
> *Content-Transfer-Encoding: ProxyBit.*
>
> *TO: J3984@i.mw.mail.com*
> *FROM: NickyYB@e.mw.mnet*
> *SUB: Melinda*
>
> *MESSAGE:*
> *Just so we're crystal, I don't plan to tell her*
> *nothing about the hit. Ain't like she's*
> *Family. So get your head out of your ass*
> *about this. I got it.*

My search on Melinda turned up dozens of articles. The laser gun used and the way her body had been tossed into the black to drift pointed to a mob hit, but police found little to link her to the Family. She'd once dated one of Junto's boys, but when she'd discovered his ties, she'd broken it off. The obituary had been brief and lacking emotion, and I skimmed through it until I reached the final line:

> *Melinda Mathis-Kerric is survived by her husband, Clay; her*
> *sister-in-law, Lissa Kerric; and her two children.*

I tagged the pages and saved them in a folder. Not only did Lissa have the ability to take out someone like Nick, she had motive as well.

Dammit, why'd she always have to complicate everything?

WHEN THE DOOR SLID OPEN TO THE COMMON AREA, MY crew awaited their turn with a galaxy between each of them. No one talked. No one shared stories about Lissa kicking the ass of some thief or Zac getting *The Perffaith* to limp along on half-baked goods 'til we hit a repair station. The only people touching were Lissa and Petrie, who held hands under the table.

"I ran a search on everyone's email accounts." Minor reactions to my statement: Lissa's jaw clenched, Zac nodded to himself, and Seb's shoulders slumped. But it was Petrie who surprised me as she bit her lip. "I know where everyone was supposed to be when we searched the *Lucky Fish* and where they said they were, but I want to hear it for myself. We'll start with Jake."

He answered as soon as I finished his name. "Was on the bridge with you, Captain."

"The entire time?" asked Lissa.

"I followed the Captain to the engine room once Zac let up a shout. Never left the Captain's side."

Zac held up a finger. "Wait, aren't you gonna tell us what you found in your search? I mean, you—"

He stopped when I gave the slight shake of my head. For the moment, the fewer who knew about my crawling into Nick's past the better. Besides, everyone but Lissa had come up clean. She was no Petrie, no jumpy woman who hid behind frumpy clothing and a microscope. Lissa didn't use her physical appearance as some women might either. Her cargo pants weren't too tight, nor was her button-up shirt undone in some lame attempt to sway opinion. Nor did she lean across the table in my direction. Instead, she leveled her gaze on me—relaxation to a T. Had she been this calm when meeting with Nick over her sister-in-law's murder?

"The data search through user account's didn't pay off. Nothing beyond the typical came up: porn, family correspondence, the regular. Lissa, retrace your steps for me," I said. A small lie but a necessary one.

"Until Seb spoke of trouble, I was standing guard outside the engine room as requested. No crew left until I escorted them back to *The Perffaith* on your orders."

"You stood outside the doors, not inside?"

"Yes, Captain."

Did you ever leave your post? Did anyone else see you there?

She must've followed along the same thought trail as she shook her head. "No one passed by until you arrived, so no one can verify my whereabouts."

A red light dangling from the ceiling blinked once more before going dark, and my officers glanced up at the sudden light shift.

"Okay, I know this is an important convo and all, but what the hell is all this crap? Besides distracting?" Zac asked as he pointed at the stained child's sock on the wall.

"I had attempted to encourage cheer through the use of items from the mythos of Saint Nicholas," whispered Seb.

Zac held the short sock up by its end. "Yeah, but what's up with the halfling stocking?"

His laughter pulled up short as Lissa spoke. "That must be yours, Zac. See? It's short like your temper."

Zac's face froze as he clenched his jaw. What used to be jokes between my crew, now caused tension. Something had broken in our group, and a few minutes' laughter wasn't gonna heal it.

The last thing I needed was a fight, so I returned to the topic at hand. "Zac, why were you coming from the cargo hold when Seb mentioned trouble?"

"I wanted to check on little Seb first. Make sure he wasn't in any trouble, being new and all and most likely to get killed walking up the stairs." Zac slapped Seb on the back.

Seb's sunglasses slid down his nose, and he winced from the lights before shoving the thick glasses back into place.

I would've said he met my gaze, but with his eyes hiding behind his sunglasses, I would've never known. Always hidden —everything about him. He didn't flinch or scowl either like I would've at Zac's ribbing. Calm as I'd never been—not since before we'd found Nick's corpse.

"He would not have discovered me in the cargo hold as I was already seeking our heat source. The cargo bay bore an enormous hole in its hull. A single crate remained, anchored to the wall. After the scanners began working, I followed the blip."

"Did anyone see you?" asked Petrie.

He shook his head. "Not until I encountered Jake and Zac."

"And you, Zac?" I asked. "Seems to me I ordered you to remain on board *The Perffaith*."

"Ain't no way I did it. By the time I got on the *Lucky Fish* and got the heat source all sorted out, I would've had no time to reach our vic," said Zac.

I shrugged. "That leaves you, Petrie-Dish."

"I was on board *The Perffaith* until Seb mentioned the corpse."

"Where on *The Perffaith*?" asked Seb. He was standing again, his mouth-flap curled back and open. "Can anyone confirm your precise location?"

"The computer can," answered Zac. "The logs show the correct time stamp for when she left Lissa's room for the *Lucky Fish.*"

Interesting. She hadn't been in the infirmary, and Zac had known it. Why'd he been digging through the logs? Seb halted his pacing to glare at Petrie.

Lissa rose when Seb stepped in Petrie's direction—a swift motion I caught out of the corner of my eye. She placed both hands on Seb's shoulders. Lissa towered over Seb and glanced down her nose to see past his shades. "If you've got a problem with Petrie's personal life, get over it. Look at her or anyone else on this ship like that again, and it won't matter that you're first mate. I'll pitch you out the ship myself," she said.

He wriggled in her grasp, but she held him firmly in place. "If you would allow me go."

"Apologize."

Seb shot me a plea for help, and I shrugged. He got himself into this; he could get himself out of it.

"My apologies, Petrie. Everyone." He stumbled back when Lissa released him.

"Captain, I think it's time for that room search. It's too easy for us to cover for one another," said Lissa.

I nodded. Maybe in our search, we'd find something tying someone to Nick, someone else. Maybe I'd figure out what had happened when Lissa had met with him.

Or maybe I'd figure out why it rattled me so much to see her kicking sideways with Petrie.

CHAPTER TEN

PETRIE'S ROOM was first on our list, if for no other reason than to shut Seb up. Everything tucked into place, her room was nearly unlived in. Dust gathered in the bottom of a laundry hamper and across the food dispenser. Bed neatly made and floor cleared of any tripping hazards. Everything in its place, unused.

She stood, arms across her chest, as Zac and I dug through what few belongings remained in the room. At the door, Seb and Lissa watched, the latter with wide stance as she guarded the doorway.

It didn't feel right to be combing through Petrie's belongings like I was, but my hands busied themselves as my mind wandered.

I almost didn't catch it, so buried was it in a wadded up shirt shoved into an otherwise empty drawer. When my fingers closed around the hard object, I sighed.

"What is it?" Zac whispered, and I opened my palm to display a capped needle.

"Safety ring's missing. I assume it's used, though it's hard to say if it was used on Santa."

In a room the size of a small shuttle, whispers carried like a baby crying. By the look on Petrie's face, she'd heard it all.

"The needle's mine, though it wasn't used on our Santa." Petrie pulled out a vial from another drawer and held it up. "Allergen serum."

"For...?" I asked.

"I'm allergic to Lissa's cat."

Seb muttered something in *Alphan* as he fled the doorway.

"Run it for DNA...On second thought," I turned and handed the needle to Jake, "have her assistant run it. Send the results to me direct."

Jake left, with Petrie closely behind. Lissa stepped on my boot heels as she followed me toward Seb's room. When I reached the door panel, it read *unlocked* and the room occupied. Lissa stood opposite me, her hand on her taser.

"Be careful, Mark," she whispered, and I arched one eyebrow. "He's been...Petrie wasn't lying when she said he's been following us. Something's off about him."

"Don't tell me you believe all that prejudicial horseshit about *Alphans*?"

"I know you don't want to hear this, but it's true. Seb believes...." She trailed off and stared at the taser in her hands. "He believes that Petrie and I are *taurists*. Evil."

I scanned the band on my wrist to announce us. "You're right, I don't want to hear about your paranoia." The same old shit as before, only it was Seb this time instead of Zac. Here I'd thought she'd changed in the past few years. "I expect you to do your job without prejudice, Lissa."

The door slid open with a faint chime. A musty odor itched my nose something fierce as I stepped inside the dark room. Seb's faint shape sat across from the door, his hand shading his exposed eyes from the hallway light. "If you do not mind, please close the door until I have my glasses," he said.

At my nod, Lissa stepped inside and allowed the door to

slide shut. We stood in near pitch darkness as Seb rummaged around to my right. A slight hiss closed a metal drawer. When the lights rose, Seb leaned against the wall donning his shades. "Please feel free to search my personal belongings. There is nothing here I wish to hide."

As I approached the wall-drawers, my nose flared at the pungent odor—like sweaty socks in a microwave. No stains along the walls, so he hadn't set any biohazard growing in my ship. The odor was definitely inside a drawer, whatever it was.

I tugged a drawer open at random, and the stench of sweat and something sour bowled over me. Lissa passed me a pair of rubber gloves, and I nodded my thanks.

Nothing hid within the "clean" laundry, but nestled inside the corner desk were three journals, each held together with a sinew-type thread down the middle.

"Please do be careful with those." His voice cracked as he spoke.

"Is that leather? Or...something else?" asked Lissa.

Touching their covers was not in my plan. No telling what skin they came from. Lissa picked one up at random, and I muttered, "I didn't know anyone still wrote on paper. If that's even paper."

Seb bobbed his head up and down. "My mother bound these journals from the hide of a *whonta* on the day of my birth. The inside pages are from the mighty *rew* tree, which stands thirty meters in height. These books will tell my life story to my offspring and their offspring."

After a few page turns, Lissa handed me a book and pointed.

03/1/2108 21:54 PM

She has remained another evening with the security officer. They carry on, right under the captain's nose, as if it would not hurt him to see his *amhon* with another. It would crush him.

How could she remain with the security officer? To be *taurists* is unforgiveable, yet she is the moon. How can I see her as such?

Is she unaware that I stood outside for ten minutes? Did I perhaps misjudge her invitation to stop by and discuss current medicinal treatments for the itching of the scalp? Perhaps she meant for me to come by another time. I must have misunderstood. She would not make such an error.

03/2/2108 09:20 AM

I cannot sleep. What am I to do? How can I love something so vile? My mother would be ashamed.

The surveillance dated back months, though his feelings were a more recent development. I snagged the other journals. Looks like I had a little light reading to do tonight.

"Will those be returned?" he asked.

"Once I've taken a look at them."

"Captain," he said, and his shades slid down his nose an inch to expose damp, dark eyes near the size of my fist. "Those —those are personal."

"So was this murder."

My wristband beeped. The DNA results were back on Nick and the needle. I swallowed hard.

"Something up?" Lissa asked.

"Later."

Other than the journals, our search of Seb's room came up empty. The *Alphan* lived an odorous and bizarre life but had nothing connecting him to Nick. Lissa's jaw clenched as we left Seb's room.

"What is it?" I asked.

"I didn't realize...I thought—"

"You thought it was something else, not a crush that had him stalking Petrie."

She nodded. "Not that stalking isn't an issue, but oddly enough, I don't think he's our murderer. He's too much of a chicken shit. Though I suppose he could've planted that needle on Petrie."

"Nope. Tests came back. Only Petrie's DNA on the needle. It was used for her allergy shots."

"Doesn't that mean Petrie's innocent?"

I leaned against the wall with a sigh. "Not necessarily. She could've tampered with her assistant's results or even those of the autopsy. Seb's not wrong on that point."

When she shook her head, the silver beads in her braids glittered in the overhead light. It was good to see her hair long again rather than the short rainfall she'd sported before. "Maybe Seb did a botched frame job? No, it has to be someone else. Why frame someone you love?"

"Maybe because you can't have them?" I asked. The door panel outside Seb's room changed to the locked signal, and I pulled Lissa away from the door. "I tend to agree with you that he's not our guy, but I can't rule him out just yet. No more than anyone else."

She must have caught the unspoken implication as she pointed in the direction of her quarters. "Let's get this over with."

"Lissa—" I followed her down the corridor. As my security officer, her quarters were next to mine: something that had once been convenient. I bit back my question.

Her room was as I remembered it—simple and without decoration. The occasional book out of place gave the room a lived in appearance but other than that, her room was as clinical and cold as Petrie's had been. The exception was the cot, which lay in the corner beneath a mess of tussled blankets. "Tell me, Lissa. Did you kill Santa?"

"No." The light-brown hand on my forearm was pale against my dark skin. "I thought you knew me better than that, Captain."

"Why Petrie?" I cursed the wrong question that had escaped me. "Never mind, I'm not sure I care to know."

She shrugged and pulled open the wall-drawers for my perusal. I dug through her belongings and swallowed back more emotion than I cared to admit when I encountered one of Petrie's polka-dotted cardigans. "Why'd you meet with our victim, Nick?"

"What?" she asked, her hand in midair. When I didn't reply, she opened her desk drawers, all of which had been locked.

A bit of digging found most of the drawers clear of evidence, and I moved to the single shelf above her cot, which was full of trophies and awards. "You met with Nick concerning the murder of your sister-in- law, Melinda. Why?"

She folded her tall frame into the padded chair in the corner with a long sigh. "Melinda's murder was a mob hit. I knew you had contacts to the Family. I bullied Zac into giving me an email address. He gave me one for a Nick Melorrey. I thought if I talked to him, he'd be able to tell me why Junto called in a hit on her. But I never met with him, not in person."

I was gonna kill Zac for tangling her up with the Family. To Lissa, I said, "That last job with Junto went way south of normal, Lissa. You almost died. In fact, you left me after that job. What in the world would possess you to get mixed up with the Family?"

"I had to know!"

The shout caught me off guard, and I shoved a wobbling trophy back onto the shelf. Her cheeks were flushed and her eyes wide.

"The police knew it was a hit, but they refused to do anything, Mark. They said Junto was untouchable. What would you have done...if it had been me? Would you've let it go?"

No. I would've buried him with my bare hands. "Did you kill Nick?" I asked.

"No. Nick wouldn't tell my anything. He wouldn't meet with me. Just sent me useless emails full of nothing. Hell, I didn't even know our victim was *that* Nick until you mentioned the mob connection earlier."

It would've been easier if I could've believed her. "So you didn't recognize him?"

"I never saw him in person. He wouldn't accept video calls either so no. It seems our victim had many names."

I closed the last of the wall-drawers. "Room's clear."

"You believe me then?"

I spun to find her all too close. She smelled like strawberries, and I leaned forward until my nose nearly touched hers.

"Is this what you came here for, Captain?" she asked, voice colder than the *Lucky Fish*.

I flinched at the door's hiss behind me, and my nose bumped hers.

"Sorry, Captain. Didn't mean to interrupt—" I winced at Zac's words.

Behind him stood the rest of my officers. Petrie bumped into Jake's shoulder when he stopped. "Why the—" Her face crumpled.

"I apologize for suggesting it, Captain, but is it possible you have a conflict of interest?" asked Seb as he brushed past Zac. He opened the wall-drawers with less care than I'd taken. With a shrug, Zac joined him while I stood there looking the idiot. Her room turned up nothing again. Seb stepped back, stray hairs from his wig sticking to his sweaty face.

"Satisfied?" asked Lissa.

Seb stumbled away from her and tripped over a chair leg..

"Since you're convinced there's something going on, we'll do the Captain's quarters next," she said.

They expected me to lead the way. I'm not sure why I didn't, only that my brain was still arguing with my heart over what the hell had just happened. Zac led the short procession ten feet over with me trailing behind like a guilty party.

Except I wasn't.

My officers watched as Zac and Seb now searched my quarters. I took a moment to stuff Seb's journals into a wall-drawer for later reading.

When Zac and Seb reached my desk, Seb's jaw pulsed. He held up a picture frame I recognized all too well. "Why do you have a photo with Santa?" he asked, and my tongue rolled across the dry roof of my mouth. I'd forgotten to return the photo to the false bottom in the wall-drawer.

The old school digital frame was passed around the crew.

Nick had said he wanted to connect, to make up for lost time while we still had it. Rather than swallow my pride and the past, I'd shut him down. And he'd given up. I might as well have killed him myself.

"Mark?"

Damn Lissa's eyes. If they could've bored black holes through me, they would've.

"I don't know why I didn't see it before." Lissa handed Petrie the wooden frame. "Look at the nose."

"Dominant arch, flared nostrils," Petrie said. "I ran DNA on our victim, Mark. I thought it a mistake, but seeing this picture..."

Zac glanced between the digital photo and me as he shifted his weight from one foot to the other. He tried to hide his *I-told-you-so* expression behind a fake sneeze and failed.

"You knew, didn't you?" Lissa asked, and Zac studied the dirt beneath his fingernails.

I said, "Leave Zac out of this. He was following orders."

"Captain, if you have a connection to the deceased, it would be best to reveal that now." Lissa paled at Petrie's comment.

I took the photo from the doctor. "His name's not Nick Johnson. It's Nick Banes, and he's my father."

Saying the words made them real.

Feet shuffled in the room, but no one spoke. When Lissa's hand touched my shoulder, I flinched. "Mark, your father was a first grade asshole. He abandoned you. I think we'd all understand if—"

"If what?" Voice too sharp, I bit my tongue. "If I snapped and killed him? I know what this looks like, but I didn't do it. Much as I would've liked to years back, this murder wasn't me."

"How'd your father end up dead on the *Lucky Fish?*" asked Jake.

"And why were you hiding this photo?" Petrie pointed at the false bottom in the wall-drawer. "No offense, but this isn't looking good for you, Captain."

There wasn't any way I was walking out of this without being gutted. The story tumbled out too fast, too raw: his scamming first my mother, then Gran; his need for money and booze; the jobs he had done for Junto; and finally, his attempt to reconnect. "He came crawling out of the meteor field to give me some line about dying or some shit. Wanted to get all enlightened with forgiveness at the mountain. That's when that photo was taken."

"And you decided to keep this hidden because?" asked Petrie.

"I wasn't hiding it. It's private and not relevant."

"Not relevant, my ass." Zac flushed. "Forgive me, Captain, but that's what we'd call a motive right there."

Swallowing proved difficult, yet I managed.

Petrie said, "But our victim *was* sick. The autopsy determined that."

"He was, but by the time he'd reached out to me, he'd told so many lies, killed so many...it didn't matter if he was being truthful. Either way, I didn't kill him. Jake was with me during the time of death. Are we done here?"

Zac nodded to Lissa, who announced, "Room's clean."

"Jake could be protecting you, Captain. It wouldn't be the first time someone from your crew kept you from the noose. That last job from Junto...." said Zac, and I could've strangled him. Zac threw up both hands. "Just laying out the facts...Captain."

His jaw clenched as he turned away from me.

"I didn't kill him," I said, but no one was listening.

The crew followed me from my quarters with mumbles and whispers, and my stomach churned. My crew'd gone from family to a maelstrom of accusations in less than forty-eight hours. A sweep of Jake's quarters turned up nothing more than the typical array of dirty laundry.

Lissa turned to Zac. "Where'd you get the idea to run salvage on this particular ship?" she asked.

His smile tightened at the edges. "We haven't had decent work in months. Not since...not since we took Seb on board. No one wants to deal with a vessel with an *Alphan*. Add in all that union crap—"

She waved her hand in the air. "Yes, yes, but how'd you find *this* job?"

"If we don't get more memory for the food replicators, we're gonna be eating like the junkies on Europa. When I saw this job come up on that board for folks looking for side-work, I figured it was a good fit. Ran it by Mark and off we went."

"Which board?" I asked.

I thought his lips would split, the painful way he over-grinned. "Side-Slide."

"Dammit, Zac. That site's quasi-legal at best."

"Yeah, well, it ain't like you've never taken the odd job to keep *The Perffaith* running."

Lissa sighed. "Did you know the site is backed by Junto?"

"Yes."

The answer was too fast in coming, too confident. Lissa and Zac. Both with motive. Both my friends.

"You just happened upon a salvage job within hours of a fight?" asked Lissa.

"Well, yeah."

I stared at Zac. Every lie he told poked a hole in the façade of calm demeanor. I was drowning in lies.

"While we're speaking of weirdness," said Zac as the crew walked to his room. "Lissa, how'd the meeting go with Nick?"

The procession halted. "Ya knew our stiff ?" asked Jake.

Lissa sighed. "Not really. I was investigating a murder—"

"So you've done this before then?" Zac smirked.

"Dammit, shut up and let me finish. I was investigating a mob hit and needed info from someone within the Family. *Zac* —" she stressed his name, "—gave me the email address for Mark's contact, a Nick Melorrey. I didn't know it was the same man, because I never met him in person. Never even had a video chat. Just emails."

"I'm sure that's all it was," said Zac.

When this was dealt with, I was gonna have a little chat with Zac. I didn't need more shit stirred on my ship.

Zac pressed his hand to his door's panel, and the lock released. "After you, Captain," he said.

Here was another room I'd visited many a time, though usually while piss-drunk. It was the only time he'd sucker me into playing a round of poker or jack. The walls held holographic images of a dozen starships, each more decadent and expensive than *The Perffaith*. Like Petrie's room, his was neat leaning on not lived in.

I'd already skimmed each crew member's log, but I pulled up Zac's for another look while Lissa rifled through the wall-drawers. Each log noted his entrance and exit from his room, none of which were particularly suspicious until the day of Nick's murder. At 08:00, he'd left his quarters for the morning. We'd all left the infirmary at 21:04, but the computer never logged Zac as returned to his room.

All of us were desperate for sleep, and knowing Zac, he'd have caught some zee-time when he could. I scrolled down and caught this morning's log. He'd left his room at 07:30.

Zac's shadow across the screen grew in size, and I closed the file. A few clicks later had me scanning his browsing history, emails, and calls.

"Feel free to enjoy my porn collection," he said and laughed. Gaps appeared in his history—moments where he'd logged into the system and done nothing. When I didn't laugh, his reflection on the screen frowned, and I forced a grin.

Something about the lack of computer data turned my stomach something fierce. In my study of the crew's logs, dozens of lines showed their movements and computer conversations in the past two days. Zac's were mostly the same except for the holes. "Zac, when did you come back to your room last night?" I asked.

"It must have been about 23:00 or so. Just after finishing my report. Actually, make that 23:15 since Lissa interviewed me toward the tail end of things."

He'd taken the bait. Now to drag the fish along until it stopped flopping. "Something odd's going on with the computer. Between this and the scanners, I wonder "

Zac cocked his head. "Think we've been hacked or something?"

"Interesting choice of words coming from a former hacker," said Lissa. When I turned away from the computer, Lissa held Zac's scanner before her. Six heat sources read in his room. "I thought you said the scanner wasn't reading right," she said.

He shrugged. "It wasn't, but I replaced the memory this morning. Been reading just fine since then."

Lissa closed her mouth at my look. Last job we'd run had left our scanners blipping when they oughta have been blooping. Damned planetary moisture had done quite a number on their innards. I'd placed the order for new parts myself, only they hadn't arrived yet.

I didn't know why, but this was a bet I'd make sober. Zac was lying to me.

CHAPTER ELEVEN

"SEEMS CONVENIENT," muttered Petrie from the doorway.

"What does?" Zac's voice was level, but he curled one hand into a half-fist.

"Your missing the heat source like that."

"Look, Petrie. I get that you're unusually gung-ho to find who killed Santa, especially if it takes the heat off of your girlfriend, but this don't mean shit. So I missed the heat source. With people blathering in their speakers at me, it's an easy mistake. Besides, Mark's dad died from CO poisoning. I still think he coulda jabbed himself with something when he felt himself go all woozy."

Seb brushed past Petrie. "Or maybe you are attempting to frame everyone for your own actions. You possess the needed knowledge to render the *Lucky Fish*'s computer silent."

"Maybe," said Zac, and he leaned nose-to-nose with Seb. "Or maybe you want it to sound that way. Since the murder, everyone's been hell-bent on accusing one another, but maybe it's just as I said. Here we are spinning our wheels over solving an accident when we could be selling our salvage. I don't know about you, Seb, but I'd like to eat something not replicated from old protein sometime this year."

Stress and lack of sleep had rendered them useless to me. I moved to step between the two, but Lissa beat me to it. "Enough," she shouted.

Before accusations started flying again, I said, "Everyone to their quarters. Let the skele-crew handle *The Perffaith*. And when I say your quarters, I mean your *own* quarters."

Petrie frowned but nodded.

"I've got to make sure the rest of the scanners are—"

I interrupted Zac with an upright hand. "I have a few leads to follow up before we finish grabbing salvage off the *Lucky Fish*. Stay in your room. Don't make me lock everyone inside."

My crew muttered as they spread out toward their quarters. Zac flopped into an empty chair, his fingers already running across the screen beside him.

"When this is all done, we're gonna have a talk, Zac."

"I'm sure," he muttered.

I followed Lissa outside and sighed when Zac's door shut behind me.

"You know something," she said.

"Possibly. Feel like helping?"

Lissa grinned and led the way to my quarters. Outside my door, she turned about-face. "I'm sorry. I should've told you about Melinda—"

"Don't," I said as I opened the door with a handprint. I locked the door behind us.

On the wall screen, I put in a call to Junto. Another hold as I waited for my message to reach the proper person, and Lissa fiddled with her sealed braid tips.

"Why are you calling him?" she whispered.

The screen twitched before Junto's mug popped up. "I thought I made it clear I don't owe you."

"You did, but I needed some information."

He furrowed his brows, then a slow smile spread across his face as he glanced over my shoulder at Lissa. "I see you two have worked things out."

I dismissed his attempts to push my buttons with a shrug. "Last time we had a chat, you said your boys were here to get the goods, yet they didn't. You and I both know you sent them to knock off Nick, but you had to ensure Nick was dead in the debris. Who'd you call on my ship to be sure?"

Junto's smile didn't falter as he wrested his attention from Lissa. "What makes ya think I did any such thing?"

"No games, Junto. If you had a mole in the Fam, you'd flush him out faster than I could toss the *Lucky Fish*. Allow me to do the same."

"What will you give me for such intel?"

It was my turn to smile. "I won't mention to the authorities where to find Melinda's killer."

"You won't, anyway. You got nothin'."

I pressed a button on my screen to forward a message his way. "In a few minutes, or maybe an hour with the way relays have been delayed, you'll get an email from Nick's email account—one where he makes very sure to state that he won't meet with Lissa here or tell her what happened to Melinda. I'm sure it could link Nick and you to her, which may open more doors than you want blown open at this point. Hell, they may find the clues in their own search of your computers there on Europa." I shrugged. "But hey, if you wanna take that risk, be my guest."

Junto's left eye twitched, but he gave the slightest nod. My account pinged. Guess he had faster mail relays than me. "Don't call again."

"I don't intend to."

The screen darkened, and I pulled up the message he'd sent. The decrypted file contained a series of video messages. Whoever our killer was had disconnected the video feed and fed the voice through the computer. A robotic voice read off the details of the hit—where, when, who—not much else.

"Dammit," I muttered.

"Open another one."

Confirmation that Junto had told someone on board about the salvage and hired them to kill Nick (*if found*), but nothing more. Another file, this one giving details of a meeting between Nick and Lissa. A meeting that never happened. At least according to her.

"That...that never happened. I didn't meet with him." She curled her fingers into fists. "You have to believe me."

"I can't."

"What are you going to do?"

"Find the proof I need. One way or another." My door slid open at my approach, and I gave her a brief nudge in its direction. "Look, just head back to your room. Stay put until I figure this out."

Lissa rested her hand against my chest—a moment's warmth in the situation's chill. "Mark—"

"Don't say it. We both know you wouldn't mean it in the morning." The words were harsh, but I couldn't trust her. Not yet. I'd ask her forgiveness later, assuming I was alive to do it.

Assuming she wasn't the murderer.

My gut clenched as she left, and I pulled up the ship's map on the door panel. Heat sensors showed the two-member skeleton crew in place while the rest were in their rooms.

I sank into my cot and pressed the button to my right. A screen slid out, and I pulled up the logs from before.

The hole from last night was gone. Zac had altered his coming and goings again. The question now was why. What was he hiding now? What had I missed? I pulled up the logs from the last twenty-four hours for Lissa's rooms, but they'd been cleared as well. He'd muddied the waters.

Maybe he was protecting Lissa. Maybe they were working together.

I scrolled away from the logs and into the command panel. The computer's line to the derelict rang true enough, but the damaged ship wasn't singing back. The *Lucky Fish* ignored my request to power up. Her computer was as lifeless as my father's corpse, which shouldn't have been the case. If nothing else, she could've piggybacked off our power. The ship's black box was intact and should've been singing one last serenade.

Maybe if I brought the black box over to *The Perffaith*, I could get it talking. I grinned at my reflection in the screen.

But first, I needed to know if Lissa had met with my father. The audio mentioned a meeting at a swank hotel in Garthus. Being all hoity-toity, maybe they'd have a record.

If I'd had to pinpoint the moment when the screen grew fuzzy, I wouldn't have been able. Only that as I stared at the small screen beside me, my vision rolled with my stomach. I blinked my way through the rocking long enough to pull up the article on carbon monoxide poisoning.

Damn.

So this was how it'd been done.

CHAPTER TWELVE

THE ROOM SPUN as I staggered to the door. The killer couldn't poison the entire ship without going down with us. If I could get to the hall— When I reached it, my door ignored my presence, and I pushed on the hand plate, which read:

LOCKED. OVERRIDE? Y/N

My finger slid across the Y, and the screen chirped a refusal. I tried to speak and couldn't. When birthdates and the names of family members didn't remove the lock, I blinked a few times while staring at the yellow glare. By the time I finished typing the L in Rachel, the world was a mix of gray haze and jagged edges. The door slid open and fresh air smacked me in the face. As I fell to my knees in the hall, I made a mental note to send the ex-girlfriend a gift of some sort. Coughs flooded the hallway as crewmembers escaped their rooms.

Jake crawled his way over to me from his room across the hall. "Need to make...sure everyone...escaped."

I nodded, but my legs refused to lift me from the floor.

Weak and quivering, I reached up and slapped my hand on a nearby panel. "Head count, please," I croaked.

Eight heat sources on board *The Perffaith.* "We're missing two."

Jake said, "The murderer. And his or her accomplice?"

"It appears to be the case." This time when I tried my legs, they held, though my stomach churned. "Check that everyone's okay. I need to get to the *Lucky Fish.*"

Jake took the left corridor while I went right. Coughs covered what little could be said as I passed by my crew members. The stairwell's door shut behind me, and I took the stairs two at a time. Two flights down, salvage from the *Lucky Fish* lay scattered across the cargo bay. In the airlock chamber, two spacesuits were missing.

Dammit. The killer was going for the black box. The remaining evidence.

My legs quivered as I pushed one foot and then the other through the legs of a spacesuit, and my fingers trembled against the zipper pull. Part of me wished I had help—Lissa's help, to be honest—but for all I knew, she'd kill me rather than help me.

The zipper moved easier than I did. Fitting the helmet in place was a relief as cleaner oxygen swept through it, and I inhaled deeply a few times before sealing off the chamber for depressurization.

Two seconds into the derelict, goosebumps crept across my skin. Wasn't much reason for it—my lone light split across her darkness as expected—but a slim one foot of metal between me and the dark embrace of space set my wiggins-radar to off the charts, especially being alone with one, possibly two killers.

If the killer was smart, he—or *she*—would be hiding in a twist of metal wreckage. Maybe both of them were stupid, hiding out in the bridge. The idea made my steps slow as I shined my flashlight's beam into every shadow between me and the evidence I needed.

Dead ahead, the sliding doors to the bridge remained pried open from our previous excursion. The suit's emergency knife wobbled in my hand as I leaned my head around the doorway.

Nothing. The bridge was empty.

One floating lap around the bridge confirmed what my eyes told my brain. The main panel lay open, and I used the lip to pull myself beneath it. Its innards were an enigma to me, but I had a hunch the dead panel wasn't from damage. Not directly. I reached behind a mess of wires until I brushed up against the manual power switch. It was switched on.

Beside it lay the reset button. Once flipped, the black box's display lit up. Lights blinked and error codes scrolled across the three inch screen for a full minute before the command prompt blinked twice. Waiting.

I noted the killer's entrance by the pop of my speaker and gripped my knife. I couldn't ignore the cold sweat inside my suit.

Zac held one hand behind his back. A weapon of some kind? I used the panel for leverage as I faced him. "Was it you?"

He didn't answer—his eyes focused on the black box.

"Why?" I asked, and he pushed himself through the doorway and into the bridge.

Zac held an old-fashioned gun in his hand. "Money." He jerked the weapon to the right, and the speaker in my helmet crackled. "Get away from the box."

"Or what? You'll shoot me?" My breath came too fast. If he destroyed the black box, all evidence would die with me. "You're my best friend, Zac. I can't believe you'd kill me for money."

"Quit stalling. I saw you come alone. No one's coming to save you."

A bead of sweat crawled its way across my chin. Where was Lissa? Had she worked with him? Or had she been a hostage?

"How do you know that thing will even work?" I nodded at his gun. "No oxygen on the ship."

He rolled his eyes. "See? This is why. This!" The gun jumped with his gestures. "You don't have the brains to climb out of a paper bag, yet you're the mighty captain of his own ship. How many times have I pulled your ass from the proverbial fire?"

"More times than I can count. Which is why you've got me wondering what this is all about."

My helmet's speaker crackled again with his answer. "You. Here I've gone and done everything you've ever asked of me, saved your life any number of times, nursed your broken heart after that bitch dumped you, and how do you repay me? Hmmm? By making some bigoted *Alphan* your first officer!"

He wasn't working with Lissa? My breath caught in my throat. Then where was she? I coughed in my helmet. Oh gods. Was she dead?

"Seb was an accident. I should've never accepted him from Junto."

Zac floated within a few feet of me. Spittle decorated the interior of his helmet, and his eyes were too large for sanity. "No shit. It should've been *me!*"

I held the knife uselessly at my side. "If you had a problem with me, why go after my father?"

Over his shoulder, a light flashed once in the corridor before fading. "I told you!" he shouted, and the gun jumped closer to my faceplate. "The money. Junto was willing to pay shiploads to make sure Nick was good and dead. You weren't going to miss him and with all that money, I'd be free of *The Perffaith.*"

I tried to focus on his face rather than the new shadow in

the hall, but the gun sent a new round of shakes through me. For whatever reason, Zac was convinced it would fire.

I held up my hands. "You were never a prisoner here, Zac. Take your money and go."

The grin that split his thin lips was full of malice. "Can't. You know too much. How'd you figure out it was me, anyway?"

A booted foot stopped within the emergency doorway behind Zac. The silver strip across the helmet matched those across our feet. One of my crew was here. I sighed with relief, but Zac misread my reaction.

"That's it? This is all I get from the mighty captain of *The Perffaith?* So much for being perfect. What would your precious Gran think of you now?"

Anger flushed my face. Despite the lack of gravity, my arms and legs moved too fast through the dimly lit bridge. I reached for Zac as the pistol's muzzle flashed. Something hit me and pain erupted across my ribcage.

I flipped the latches of Zac's helmet, releasing the pressure seal. His mouth opened but whatever he said was lost with the lack of oxygen.

Lissa brushed past him. When she reached me, she slapped a glob of sealant across the hole in my suit. "Can you breathe? Did the bullet penetrate?"

My helmet occluded my view of my middle. "I don't think it penetrated completely. Suit's too thick. Though I think I bruised a rib or three."

As I spoke, she held up my arm to check gauges and sensor readings. "The sealant should hold long enough to get you back on the ship, but we need to leave now."

"What about him?"

I didn't want to look at Zac. I stared at the floor while my ribcage throbbed.

"Don't look," she whispered. "We need the black box."

Lissa tugged at my arm to get me moving. "Can you access it from *The Perffaith?*"

Zac's feet drifted past my view of the floor. "Yes, now that its power is on."

We drifted through the *Lucky Fish*'s dark corridors in silence. My face grew warm as fog coated the interior of my helmet. The airlock chamber stood ten feet at most, and my arm trembled as I pushed away from the wall.

"Liss..."

Her open mouth swam in the red tint of my vision, and I closed my eyes.

CHAPTER THIRTEEN

THE OVERHEAD LIGHT doubled in brightness, and I winced. "Somebody do somethin' about that light," I said, or I tried to say, but the first few words were more a croak than actual speech.

"Sit tight, Captain. Sip this." Petrie placed a straw against my cracked lips.

The water burned going down, yet soothed the back of my throat. This time when I opened my eyes, the light was less harsh, though my tear ducts worked overtime.

"What happened?" I asked. "Lissa—"

A hand squeezed mine, and when I turned my head, she sat beside me in the infirmary. Too many wrinkles lined her face. "The bullet didn't reach you, but it tore enough of a hole to cause problems."

"You patched it."

"Not enough. There was a pressure loss, enough that—" Her voice cracked, and she paused. "We almost lost you."

Several crew members waved at me from the view screen to my left. Petrie swiped them away and pulled up a list of numbers and diagrams. "Your blood was trying to boil its way out of your body," she said and injected something into my IV. "While the bullet didn't tear through the entire suit, you still bruised your ribs. You'll need to stay here overnight for observation. You're dehydrated and need the increased oxygen. "

"How long was I out?"

"A few hours. You came out of the hyperbaric tube half an hour ago."

Whatever she'd stuck in the line made the world prettier than I remembered, and I smiled at the fuzzy warmth.

"That's my Petrie-Dish." I tilted my head toward my security officer. "And my Lissa. Always looking out for me."

The former smirked while the latter frowned.

I didn't care so long as they were both beside me.

CHAPTER FOURTEEN

"CAREFUL NOW," Petrie said.

I waved her away. "Doc, I'm fine. All patched up. Walking and talking even." I allowed my legs to wobble, and many arms reached out to catch me.

When I laughed, Lissa lobbed a punch at my shoulder. "That's not funny, Captain."

I chuckled harder as they escorted me to the common area. Everyone stopped outside the door, and Lissa waved her hand. "Captain's first."

The door slid open, and when I stepped into the room, my eyes watered at the assault of lights. Greens and reds and whites twinkled, and a potted ivy sat in the corner. Someone, or perhaps several someones, had perched a flameless candle in the pot. Some damned fool had painted the thing a merry set of red and green stripes. The socks hanging across the wall were full of lumps and bumps, and a small box sat at the ivy's base.

"What's all this now?" I asked, and Seb grinned.

"Christmas!"

There was a hole in the wall where the shortest sock had

been. Zac's. Lissa caught my frown and said, "We burned it, along with his body. While you were recovering, we blew up what remained of the *Lucky Fish*."

My strength left me, and I stumbled. Jake shoved a chair under me, and I fell into it. "But—"

"Don't worry, we stripped her bare first. We got the black box data, too," she said and patted my arm. "It was a good haul all things considered. We should be able to get some fresh food at the next fueling station."

Seb picked up the small box and handed it to me. "Happy Christmas!"

Someone, probably Seb by the way he grinned, had bundled the box with a shirt and tied a silly knot at the top. My fingers fumbled with the thin rope until Lissa took pity on me and cut the fool thing.

"It is not fresh food, but perhaps you will find it equally enjoyable," said Seb.

Inside the box was the snow globe.

The twinkling lights overhead reflected off the flakes inside making them dance. I stared at it while my vision did a little dance of its own. "Damn dust on this ship. Time to cycle the air again," I said as I wiped my eyes with the back of my hand.

Lissa handed me a tissue. "We found it in...in Zac's quarters. We figured you'd want it, seeing how it was your father's."

"Thanks. What'd you find on the black box?"

The crew, who'd been digging through their "stockings" full of vitamin-candy, ceased moving at my question. Lissa took a deep breath and answered. "Junto admitted to paying Zac 500,000 credits to kill your father, though Junto wasn't the only one looking for him. He was wanted by the Family of Europa as well as crime syndicates in three other systems. Looks like this Santa thing was one of his covers. When Junto put out his request, Zac promised the Family he'd take care of him in exchange for the cash and a ship of his own."

"How'd you pull that info out of Junto?"

Lissa glanced at Petrie. "I made a deal."

I tried to stand and failed.

"I never said *I* wouldn't alert the authorities," she said and I laughed. "The black box contained brief notes from the captain of the *Lucky Fish*. It seems he bought Nick's cover story and tried to protect him from Junto's boys. The captain hid him in that closet. Some protective shelter, I guess. It had its own oxygen system, which is how Nick survived post-battle. Gave him a shot of adrenaline to keep him going in the cold when the heat went out on the *Lucky Fish*. Junto's boys couldn't find him because their ship was too damaged in the fight."

I asked, "How'd Zac know about the request?"

"He's been on Junto's radar for a while. Managed to snake a long list of jobs out of Junto that were shunted our way so Zac could perform side-jobs for the Family. When we arrived at the *Lucky Fish*, he found a single life source on board. The one Junto said might be there. We had the new scanners, so we picked up what 'the boys' had not. Zac hacked the *Lucky Fish*'s computer and flooded the safe room with carbon monoxide."

Seb curled his hands into fists around his empty sock. "And while we were chasing salvage, he set the controller back to confuse the investigation. He may have succeeded had I not found the body."

"Junto knew we were in the sector, so it was the perfect opportunity to do what his boys had failed to do," said Lissa.

I swallowed the lump in my throat. "All this because he wanted to be First Officer. Felt like I'd slighted him."

"Is that what he told you?" Lissa asked.

I nodded.

"How did you deduce he was the murderer?" asked Seb.

"Little things weren't adding up. The scanner that suddenly didn't work when it did, the logs that were too perfect, the salvage job when we needed it most. The helmets crackling and such. We'd just replaced them— seemed weird to have them malfunctioning only when we needed to communicate most. I'm embarrassed to say this, but the black box of the *Lucky Fish* should have been a red flag. Even in a damaged ship, we should've been able to pull something from it, yet we got no response. Zac had cut all reserve power to it. I had to hit the manual reset button to restore it after reconnecting it. All the info from Junto helped point me in the right direction. Suppose I owe him for that."

I flicked a peppermint across the table where it glanced off Petrie's arm. She stared at the cellophane wrapper a moment too long before she met my gaze. "He reproduced the methods and tried to kill us all in our rooms. Only two people on the ship could do that—the captain and—"

"—Someone able to hack the computer. Our killer," I said. Little piles of candy were strewn across the table, but we sat silently while the red and green lights made pretty patterns on the wall.

I stood up in a rush and clapped my hands together. "Look, Zac was bitter and angry about change. I don't know about you, but I can't spend my time looking over my shoulder for the what if 's and why's. No more jealousy and stalking people and the like. If you've gotta beef, say it. If you can't say it to me, say it to someone. We're supposed to be a family here."

My gaze crossed Seb's and he gave a brief nod of his head. He'd need watching still, especially if he was reporting back to Junto...

Jake grinned and held up a small flask. "I agree, Captain. I say we celebrate the holiday with a quart of my uncle's finest."

"Finest what?" Petrie asked as she sniffed the proffered container. "Is that intended to be drinkable?"

Jake set glasses on the table, and my medic poured a splash or two into each one.

"I propose a toast," said Seb, and he held up his glass. "That is what you do on Earth, is it not?"

The crew laughed as five glasses glittered, though from the overhead lights or the uncle's alcohol, I couldn't say.

"A toast then," said Lissa. Several glasses clanked too early, and Jake held his side with one hand as he laughed. Desperation might have driven us to it, but under the programmed Christmas lights, we were alive and grateful. "To our captain, who brought us all together."

"And to Father Christmas!" Seb shouted.

"To Father Christmas," they echoed.

"Here's to you, Dad," I whispered.

The booze burned like three suns going down, and Lissa hooted. "Happy Christmas indeed! You got any more of that stuff, Jake?"

"I do! My Christmas present to each of you, I guess."

"Did I ever tell you about how I met our great captain?" Lissa said.

I groaned. There wasn't enough hooch in the galaxy to keep my ears from burning through this story, but I grinned anyway and took another drink.

I was with the only family that mattered, and it was a happy Christmas indeed.

AFTERWORD

I've always had a fascination with the absurd, which is probably why I enjoy British TV so much. When trying to think of a holiday story, I thought, what's more absurd than Santa being part of the Mob? Mob-Santa being murdered in space! Also, who hasn't had a holiday get-together with family that went horribly wrong?

I wrote this after reading *And Then There Were None* by Agatha Christie. I loved the idea of an enclosed space mystery, especially since they devolve into everyone pointing the finger at one another.

It's similar to "The Monsters are Due on Maple Street" by Rod Serling in that regard, which is another of my favorites.

What can I say? I've always enjoyed a good episode of *The Twilight Zone*.

Raven Oak

ACKNOWLEDGMENTS

I would like to thank the many people whose hands touched this story in some way, including my editor, Mimi the "Grammar Chick;" alpha readers Maia Chance, Janine Southard, and Gayle Clemans; and other folks who read early drafts during stressful times.

I also have many thanks to send to the *Ladies of the Write* (especially Kat Richardson) for their copious and detailed suggestions; to Editor Claire Eddy & the Cascade Writers for their copious feedback. I also send copious thanks to my readers, friends, family, and last but not least, my partner, Erk.

Photo by St. Photography Studios

Multi-international award-winning speculative fiction author Raven Oak is best known for **Amaskan's Blood** (2016 Ozma Fantasy Award Winner, Epic Awards Finalist, & Reader's Choice Award Winner), **Amaskan's War** (2018 UK Wishing Award YA Finalist), and **Class-M Exile**. She also has many published over a dozen short stories in anthologies and magazines. She's even published on the moon! (No, really!) Raven spent most of her K-12 education doodling stories and 500 page monstrosities that are forever locked away in a filing cabinet.

Besides being a writer and artist, she's a geeky, disabled ENBY who enjoys getting her game on with tabletop games, indulging in cartography and art, or staring at the ocean. She lives in the Seattle area with her partner, and their three kitties who enjoy lounging across the keyboard when writing deadlines approach. Her hair color changes as often as her bio does, and you can find her at **www.ravenoak.net**.

You can *Join the Conspiracy*, her official mailing list to gain information and freebies at http://www.ravenoak.net/for-readers/mailing-list/ Besides her website, Raven Oak can be found online at the following:

facebook.com/authorroak

twitter.com/raven_oak

instagram.com/author_raven_oak

goodreads.com/raven_oak

linkedin.com/in/ravenoak1

ALSO BY RAVEN OAK

The Boahim Universe

Amaskan's Blood

Amaskan's War

*Amaskan's Honor**

*Ear to Ear**

The Xersian Struggle Universe

*The Eldest Silence**

Class-M Exile

Stand-Alone Works

Ol' St. Nick

The Ringers

From the Worlds of Raven Oak: A Coloring Book

Hungry

The Loss of Luna

Peace Be With You Friend

Anthologies

"Drip" in *99 Tiny Terrors* (Pulse Publishing)

"Weightless" in *The Great Beyond Anthology* (BDL Press)

"Scout's Honor" in *The Last Cities of Earth* (Sturgeon Press)

"Amaskan" in *Hidden Magic* (Magical Mayhem Press)

"Pretty Poison" in *Wayward Magic* (Magical Mayhem Press)

"Honor After All" in *Forgotten Magic* (Magical Mayhem Press)

"Alive" in *Swords, Sorcery, & Self-Rescuing Damsels* (Clockwork Dragon Press)

"Mirror Me" in *Unveiled Magic* (Creative Alchemy Inc.)

Reprint published in *Mercedes Lackey Fantasy Quarterly Magazine, Issue 0* (Pulse Publishing)

"Ol' St. Nick" and "The Ringers" in *Joy to the Worlds: Mysterious Speculative Fiction for the Holidays* (Grey Sun Press)

"Q-Be" in *Untethered: A Magic iPhone Anthology* (Cantina Publishing)

* Forthcoming

LIKE WHAT YOU'VE READ?

Word of mouth is the number one **best** way to ensure that your favorite authors have continued success—better than any paid advertisement.

If you enjoyed this book, please consider leaving a **review** or starred ranking on Amazon, Barnes & Noble, Goodreads, and other retail or reviewer sites.

Your review is greatly appreciated.

www.ingramcontent.com/pod-product-compliance
Lightning Source LLC
Chambersburg PA
CBHW071949190726

48293CB00004B/1412